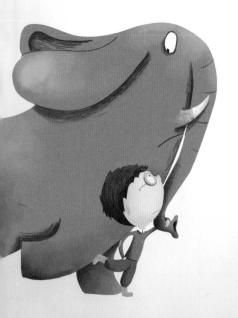

THROUGH THE ELEPHANT'S DOOR

HÉLÈNE DE BLOIS

FRANCE CORMIER

TRANSLATED FROM FRENCH
BY SOPHIE B. WATSON

ORCA BOOK PUBLISHERS

Cataloguing in Publication information available from Library and Archives Canada

Issued in print and electronic formats.
ISBN 978-1-4598-2193-4 (hardcover).—ISBN 978-1-4598-2195-8 (pdf).—ISBN 978-1-4598-2196-5 (epub)

Simultaneously published in Canada and the United States in 2019
Library of Congress Control Number: 2018954104

Summary: A young child takes his elephant on a trip to the museum, where they are closely followed by a suspicious guard.

Orca Book Publishers is dedicated to preserving the environment and has printed this book on Forest Stewardship Council® certified paper.

Orca Book Publishers gratefully acknowledges the support for its publishing programs provided by the following agencies: the Government of Canada, the Canada Council for the Arts and the Province of British Columbia through the BC Arts Council and the Book Publishing Tax Credit.

We acknowledge the financial support of the Government of Canada through the National Translation Program for Book Publishing, an initiative of the *Roadmap for Canada's Official Languages 2013-2018: Education, Immigration, Communities*, for our translation activities.

Cover and interior artwork by France Cormier
English translation edited by Liz Kemp

ORCA BOOK PUBLISHERS
orcabook.com

Printed and bound in China.

22 21 20 19 • 4 3 2 1

FOR FRIENDSHIP

—*Hélène*

FOR MY FATHER, 1925–2017

—*France*

@stained
noted
5/25/22

It was raining that morning, so I said to Émile,
"Hey, should we go to the museum?"

Émile would have loved to be able to go in through the grown-ups' entrance or even the children's entrance (because, of course, there was one). He dreamed of sneaking in just like a mouse, unseen and unnoticed. But when your waist is as big as a truck and your legs are like tree trunks, you don't have much choice. You go into the museum through the huge, the colossal, the monumental door...for deliveries.

MUSE

MUSEUM

"Not so fast, sweetie pie!"

cried the guard, seeing us come in. "You know the rules?"

I scrambled to answer. "Of course, sir! We mustn't break anything!"

The guard looked unimpressed. "And what else?"

"Um…"

CLOAKROOM

TICKETS

The guard furrowed his brow and flared his nostrils.
He said, "We don't shout, and we don't run. We don't play
hide-and-seek, nor do we play zombie tag. And, especially,
we do not touch *anything*.

Understood ?"

Émile and I nodded a polite *of course*.
And arm in trunk, we walked into the
main gallery.

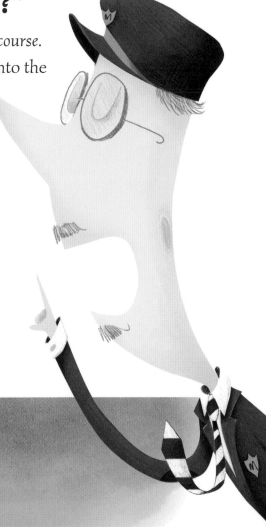

PAINTINGS

The walls of the gallery looked like a party. Each canvas overflowed with shapes and colors. Here, red squares exploded with bursts of yellow. Over there, green triangles flanked pink ones. Farther along was a bouquet of diamonds colored mauve, orange and fuchsia. It was a real carnival!

But we remembered the rules. We did not scream or run or dance the salsa. We stayed calm. We strolled about quietly, me with my hands in my pockets, Émile with his ears flapping, both of our hearts soaring like butterflies.

And then we saw it. It was a funny kind of painting. All blue and very wide. You might have said it was a piece of sky hanging at eye level. Or it could have been the sea. Or a small glimpse of paradise. The little plaque read *Blue Rectangle on Blue Background*.

Intrigued, we went in closer. Where did the blue background start? Where did the rectangle finish? We squinted our eyes, and then we opened them as wide as they would go, but we still couldn't see the shape. We inched closer…

There we were, a few centimeters from the canvas, looking for the hidden rectangle in the background of the picture, when a voice made us jump.

"Back up!"

It was the guard. Nuts! He must have been following us.

"That painting is worth a fortune!" he explained with a frown. "It's a masterpiece, unique, one of a kind. So you can look at it, but from a safe distance!"

Addressing Émile, he added, "Especially you, with those windmill ears!"

My friend turned as red as a tomato as he tucked his ears behind his head.

Émile doesn't like to talk about his ears. Especially if they are being compared to windmills. It's true his ears are big. They're huge, massive, mega, ginormous. And when he's too warm, he shakes them to cool off. They are like fans. Not windmills! That's what I should have said to the guard.

But he had already turned and gone.

I stretched my hand out to my friend. "Come on, Émile."
And we moved into the room with the big totem pole.

Carved from one giant tree, a totem rose in the middle of the room. It was so tall, so imposing, that even Émile seemed small in comparison. But the most intriguing part of it was the animals. On top sat a sculpted black crow with multicolored wings. The crow was perched on a white wolf, which was perched on a flying sturgeon, which was balancing on an acrobatic beaver standing on the shoulders of a bear. Émile and I loved that crow and all her animal friends. But the bear! Such strength! Such courage! She was supporting those other animals all by herself.

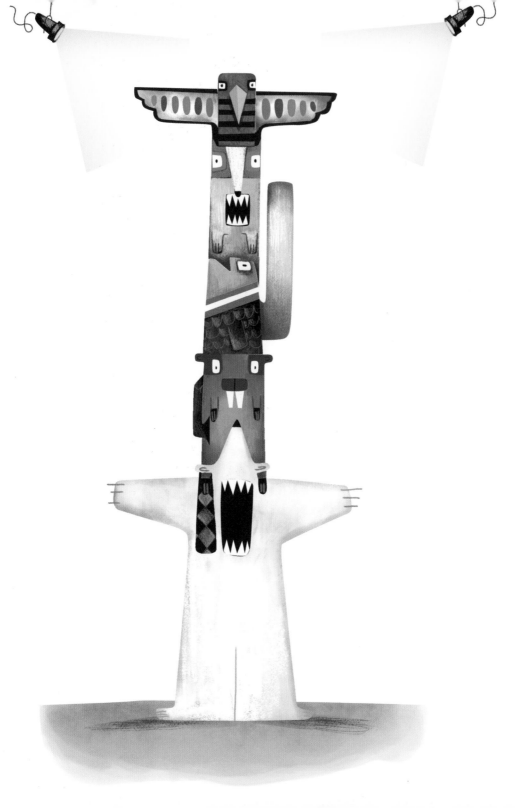

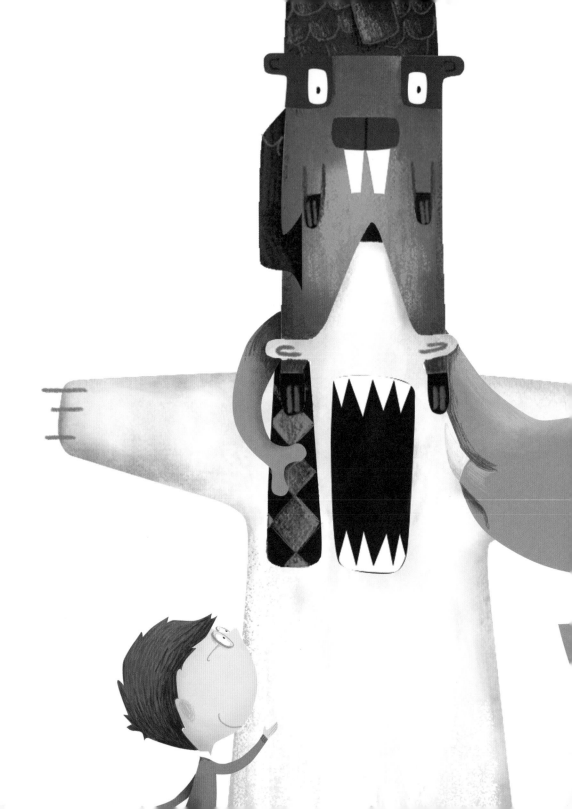

Émile, a little shy, moved toward her.

"Ooooooooooooh!"

He stretched his trunk and started sniffing. Then gently, with immense tenderness, he hugged her like an old friend. I started to come closer. I wanted to cuddle with the bear too. But I suddenly changed my mind.

"No touching!"

The guard was back.

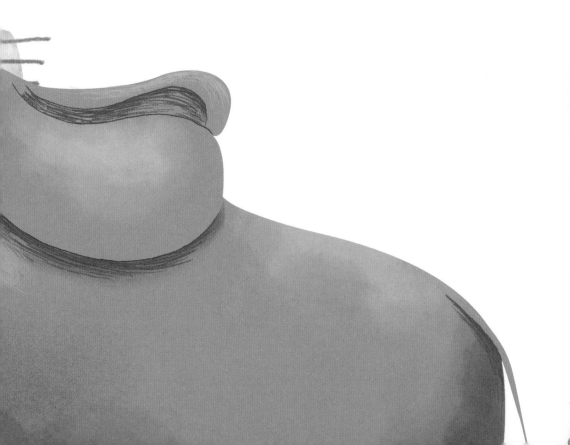

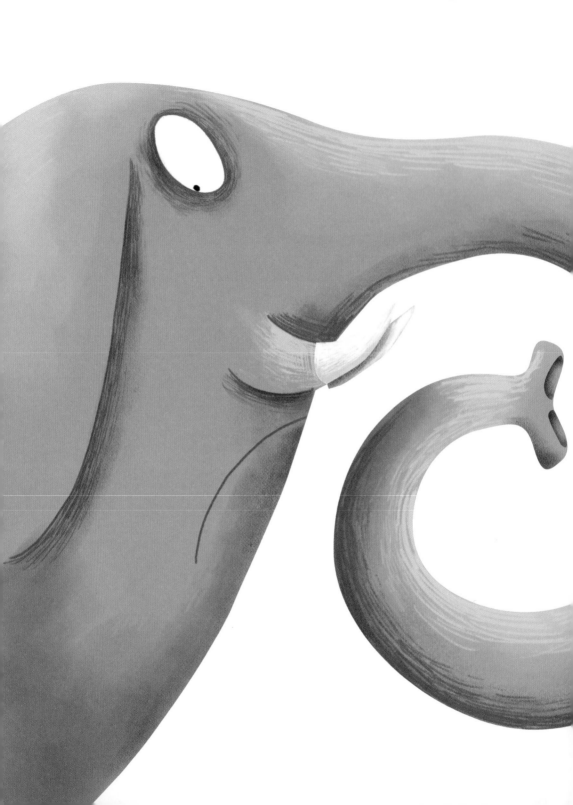

"Don't you know how to read? It's written there, there and there."

NO TOUCHING

Émile loosened his grip and tucked his trunk under his tummy, as far from sight as possible. But he didn't blush. Not this time. Instead he lowered his eyes and fixed them on the tiled floor.

But the guard was undaunted. He looked Émile over from top to bottom, then muttered, "If this fella sneezed…oof! With a trunk like that, we'd be here for months cleaning up!"

This guard was nuts! A trunk like Émile's full of snot? An elephant's trunk is more like a mighty arm, capable of uprooting a tree. Sometimes it's like a delicate hand that can carry a paintbrush, or like a fountain shooting water toward the sky. Obviously there's more to that trunk than being a nose for sneezing! This time the guard was going to hear what I had to say.

But he had already walked away from us, grumbling.

I tapped my friend's shoulder. "Don't worry about it, Émile. Come on…"

And we moved on to the ceramics room.

We had only just walked in when we heard a cry behind us.

"Nooooooooooooo!"

The guard's arms were in the air, and he was waving them about.

"But-but-but-but-but-but…"

He looked panicky.

"You can't do this! Tell me I am dreaming! Who let you in *here*?"

It's true that the room was full of precious and fragile objects—vases, plates, miniature figurines…But so what? We weren't gorillas. We knew how to be careful.

"Don't worry, sir," I reassured him. "We will be super careful. Won't we, Émile?"

The guard pulled himself together and declared, hands on his hips, "You, my little friend, are fine. It's him—"

He pointed a furious finger toward my friend.
"Him with the—with the—behind…"

Émile flinched. I stopped breathing.

"…that's as big as a mountain!"

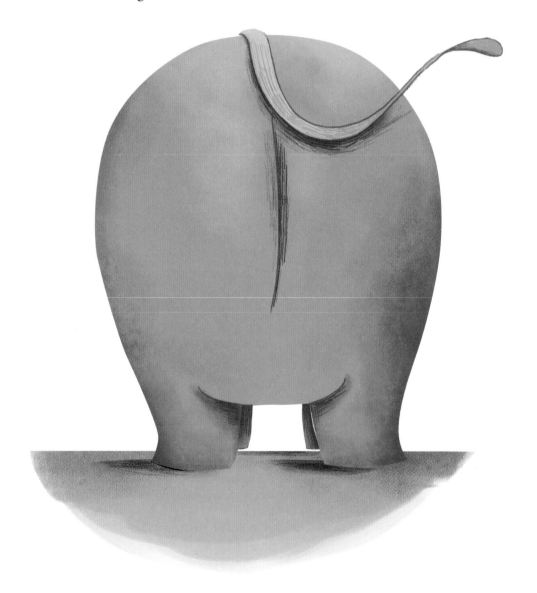

My friend turned as pale as a sheet. And me? Nuts!
Again, I didn't say a word. What could anybody say to
such an insult? Comparing his butt to a mountain! If
you were going to exaggerate, why not use the moon?
I clenched my fists. I was going to stand up for Émile,
I swear. But I had barely opened my mouth when the
guard got up on his high horse again.

"Listen, you two! The smallest scratch on the tiniest plate, and it's over. I will throw you out so fast. And good riddance! You will never set foot in this museum again. Do you hear me? **NEVER!"**

Then he turned and left us there, in the middle of the ceramics.

The big guy let out a long sigh.

I cleared my throat. "Are you okay, Émile?"

A tear rolled down his cheek. No, he was not okay.

That's when a terrible thing happened. The lights went out! All at once. We were plunged into total darkness.

"Nothing to worry about," I said. "I'm sure it's just a power outage. The lights will come on in a minute or two."

Minutes passed. The lights did not come back on. It was darker than the bottom of a well.

"What should we do, Émile?
Should we try to find the exit?"

At that moment another and even more terrible thing happened. We heard something crash to the ground.

CRAAASHHHH!

And then:

"Idiot! Someone will hear us!"

"It's the painting's fault—it's too long."

We stood as still as possible. Who were these two people whispering in the dark?

The first one said, "Watch where you put your feet!"

The other replied, "Really great idea, cutting off the electricity!"

The first one said, "Dummy! How could we have stolen the picture without being seen, huh?"

Suddenly I was even more afraid. These men were burglars!

The criminals must have heard us, because one of them shone his flashlight straight at Émile.

"Do you see what I see?"

"Don't worry about it," replied his associate, turning on his own flashlight. "He's stuffed."

And he took a step toward my friend.
"Funny-looking elephant all the same."

The other man came closer too.
"Are you sure he's stuffed?"

"Of course! He's all wrinkly."

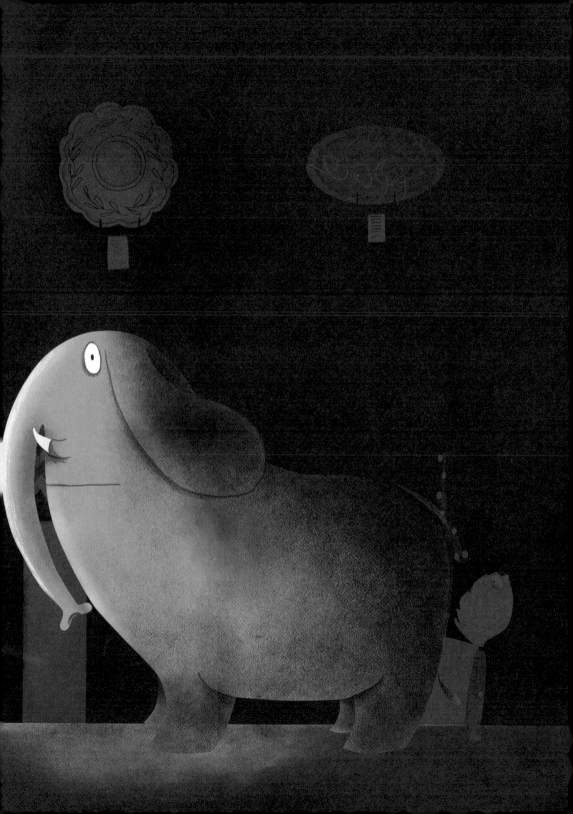

Luckily, Émile played the role of a stuffed animal really well. He didn't move a single hair. He barely breathed. But the burglars crept closer.

"Maybe it's a mammoth?"

"Or a mastodon?"

I had broken into a cold sweat. Each time the burglars opened their mouths, they took another step closer.

"Either way, he's strong."

Step.

"Is he ever strong!"

Another step.

"And his legs. Have you seen how thick his legs are?"

Nuts! They were still coming closer. Soon they'd be able to smell Émile's breath, his warm, *alive* breath. Even worse, they'd find me, hiding just behind my friend, trembling like a leaf, absolutely terrified. They'd catch me and string me up like a sausage. Or maybe they'd attack me with their flashlights.

Suddenly Émile had had enough.
He'd had enough of pretending to
be a museum statue. Enough of
sucking in his stomach and holding
still. Enough of trying to make
himself smaller and smaller, as if
he'd eventually disappear into the
floor. He needed to take a deep
breath, to stretch his spine, to take
up some space…

And then there was mayhem. Émile
unfurled his huge ears. Just like
that, without letting out a peep.
He adjusted his giant head. Raised
his trunk up high…and let out a
terrible roar.

BROOOOO

Terrified, the burglars screamed. They dropped their flashlights and started running. At least I think they did. I heard racing footsteps, and vases and plates crashing to the ground.

CRASH!

SMASH!

BOOM!

Then the sound of a collision.

BANG!

And another.

BANG!

And then nothing. It was silence and darkness.

The lights came back on, and the guard appeared. There were broken ceramics everywhere. "I knew it! I knew it! They destroyed everything."

But when he saw the two burglars lying on the floor, the guard was silent. It seemed that while trying to escape, the criminals had missed the exit and crashed straight into the wall. They were lying among shards of porcelain, the big blue painting sitting at their feet as if a giant piece of sky had dropped on top of them. All the police had to do was come and gather them up.

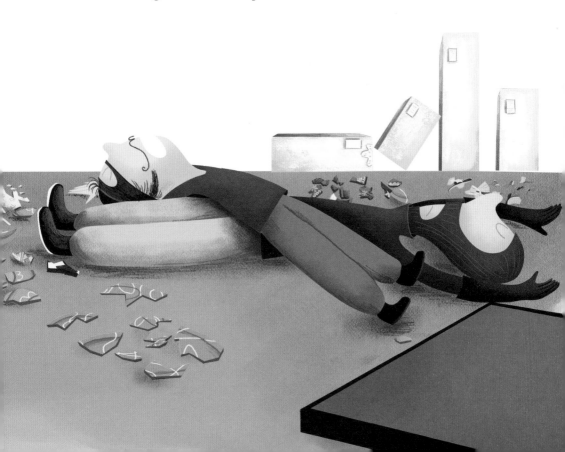

I threw my arms in the air. "Émile is a hero!" The guard stared at me, totally baffled.

"Exactly," I continued. "Because of his ears. Or thanks to his ears! His big, beautiful elephant ears. And his mighty, booming trunk!"

"BRROOOOOOOOOOOA!"

said Émile, just to show the guard what he was capable of.

Slightly more quietly I said, "Also maybe thanks to his big butt, but I can't be sure of that. It was pretty dark."

The guard nodded his head slowly. He understood.

So that's how our visit to the museum ended. The guard, acting all sweet and sugary, kindly walked us to the exit. He apologized a hundred times and acknowledged that without my brave friend, who knew what would have happened to the famous *Blue Rectangle on Blue Background?* And guess what? The guard even made us promise to come back!

"You mustn't miss the mummy exhibit. It's fabulous!"

Ever since that day, Émile doesn't want to go in through the kids' door. And the grown-ups' door? He doesn't even look at it. So what do you think? When your waist is as big as a truck and your legs are like tree trunks, you lift up your head, flap your ears and, with a confident step, choose the immense, the colossal, the ginormous door—

for elephants!!

HÉLÈNE DE BLOIS did her BA in French literature at the Université de Montréal and in dramatic arts at the Université du Québec à Montréal. In 1999 she published her first book for children, *Un train pour Kénogami*, which was a finalist for the Prix Cécile-Gagnon. Ever since, she's been writing and visiting students, encouraging the imaginations of young readers through reading, writing and art. Hélène lives in Montreal, Quebec. For more information, visit helenedeblois.com.

FRANCE CORMIER has been drawing forever. In elementary school she used to wear out her crayons and refused to play with dolls. After a first career as a landscape architect, she now devotes herself completely to illustrating playful, slightly twisted worlds full of humor. France lives in Gatineau, Quebec.